Miss Bindergarten Celebrates the Last Day of Kindergarten

by JOSEPH SLATE

illustrated by ASHLEY WOLFF

Dutton Children's Books

DUTTON CHILDREN'S BOOKS
A division of Penguin Young Readers Group

Published by the Penguin Group
Penguin Group (USA) Inc., 375 Hudson Street, New York, New York 10014, U.S.A. · Penguin Group (Canada), 90 Eglinton Avenue East, Suite 700, Toronto, Ontario, Canada M4P 2Y3 (a division of Pearson Penguin Canada Inc.) · Penguin Books Ltd, 80 Strand, London WC2R 0RL, England · Penguin Ireland, 25 St Stephen's Green, Dublin 2, Ireland (a division of Penguin Books Ltd) · Penguin Group (Australia), 250 Camberwell Road, Camberwell, Victoria 3124, Australia (a division of Pearson Australia Group Pty Ltd) · Penguin Books India Pvt Ltd, 11 Community Centre, Panchsheel Park, New Delhi—110 017, India · Penguin Group (NZ), Cnr Airborne and Rosedale Roads, Albany, Auckland 1310, New Zealand (a division of Pearson New Zealand Ltd) · Penguin Books (South Africa) (Pty) Ltd, 24 Sturdee Avenue, Rosebank, Johannesburg 2196, South Africa · Penguin Books Ltd, Registered Offices: 80 Strand, London WC2R 0RL, England

Library of Congress Cataloging-in-Publication Data
Slate, Joseph.
Miss Bindergarten celebrates the last day of kindergarten / by Joseph Slate ; illustrated by Ashley Wolff.
p. cm.
Summary: Miss Bindergarten and her class celebrate the last day of kindergarten with a party and good wishes.
ISBN 0-525-47744-6 (hardcover)
[1. Kindergarten—Fiction. 2. Schools—Fiction. 3. Teachers—Fiction.] I. Wolff, Ashley, ill. II. Title.
PZ7.S6289Mh 2005
[E]—dc22 2005009448

Published in the United States by Dutton Children's Books,
a division of Penguin Young Readers Group
345 Hudson Street, New York, New York 10014
www.penguin.com/youngreaders

Manufactured in China · First Edition
3 5 7 9 10 8 6 4

For Becky Watson of Camp Hill, Alabama, and all the kindergarten teachers who contributed ideas for this book. And the children who wanted it.
—J.S.

My heartfelt thanks to Joe and to all the generous kindergarten teachers and students who helped me bring these books to life.
—A.W.

It's the last day
of kindergarten,
and—
oh, oh, oh!—

Adam brings carnations.

Miss Bindergarten celebrates

the last day of kindergarten.

Danny scrubs a table.

Emily hands back rocks.

Franny clears her bin and shouts,
"Oh no—three smelly socks!"

Miss Bindergarten celebrates

the last day of kindergarten.

Gwen collects the building blocks.

Henry packs them away.

Ian hides beneath the desk.
"I really want to stay."

the last day of kindergarten.

Matty sets up a sprinkler. Noah connects the hose.

Ophelia tries to take a drink and gets squirted in the nose.

Miss Bindergarten celebrates

the last day of kindergarten.

Patricia passes pizza.

Quentin says, "Cheese, please."

Raffie's pepperoni slices balance on his knees.

Miss Bindergarten celebrates

the last day of kindergarten.

Sara signs a memory book.
Tommy prints "Good luck."

Ursula tells about their trip to see a fire truck.

avier gets a ribbon
for perfect class attendance.

the last day of kindergarten.

Yolanda yells, "We love you!"

Zach gives a cheer.

"Goodbye, kindergarten," says Miss B.

"It's been a special year."

"**H**ere's a little gift for you,
a penny and a Kiss.

The penny for success to come,
the Kiss that you'll be missed."

Miss Bindergarten says

goodbye to kindergarten.